Jets

Monty Must be Magic!

Colin West

Collins

Have you read all the Monty books?

Monty, the Dog who Wears Glasses
Monty - Up to his Neck in Trouble
Monty Bites Back
Monty Ahoy

First published in Great Britain by
A & C Black (Publishers) Ltd. in 1992.
First published by Young Lions in 1993
and reprinted by Collins in 1995.

10 9 8 7 6 5 4 3

Collins is an imprint of HarperCollins*Publishers* Ltd,
77-85 Fulham Palace Road,
Hammersmith, London W6 8JB.

Printed and bound in Great Britain by
HarperCollins Manufacturing, Glasgow

000 674695 0

Monty goes Missing

One morning Monty, the dog who wears glasses, wanted to find some peace and quiet.

It wasn't easy with Josie practising her recorder . . .

Mr Sprod fixing a shelf . . .

Simon watching TV . . .

and Mrs Sprod vacuuming.

Monty tried burying his head under
his blanket.

But it didn't do any good.
Then he turned his basket
upside down and crawled inside.

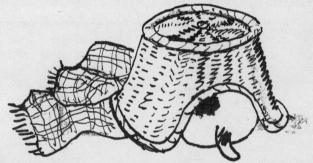

But it was still as noisy as ever.

'Maybe it's quieter outside,'
thought Monty.

He slipped out of the back door and
wandered down the garden path.

The door of the shed was ajar,
so Monty went inside.

The garden shed was nice and quiet.

Monty found some old sacks.

He snuggled down and soon
dozed off.

Meanwhile, back in the house,
everyone had finished what they'd
been doing . . .

Josie noticed Monty's basket was
upside down, and his blanket was
in a heap on the floor.

'Monty's missing!' Josie told the others. 'His basket's empty.'

They looked all over for him.

But no one could find Monty
anywhere in the house.

Maybe he's been kidnapped!

Don't you mean 'dognapped'?

He could be miles away by now.

Maybe he's run away!

Maybe he's lost his memory!

We'll have to organise a search party.

Simon suggested putting up posters
round the neighbourhood:

MISSING!
Reward for safe
return of Monty.

Contact any of
the Sprods.

Have YOU
seen this dog?

If so, please
phone 73853

WANTED!

MONTY,
the canine who
sports specs.

Meanwhile, in the garden shed,
Monty had enjoyed a peaceful nap.
He yawned and opened an eye.
It was dark.

Monty got up and sleepily waddled
back to the house.

As Monty went inside, Josie let out a squeal of delight.

Monty couldn't understand what all the fuss was about.

Everyone crowded round.

Mrs Sprod made up Monty's bed
and ordered everyone to leave him
in peace and quiet.

Monty gets the Blame

One Friday Mr Sprod's mother came to stay for the weekend.

Monty and Granny Sprod have quite a lot in common.

For instance –
they both
like afternoon
naps . . .

. . . they
both like
the same
food . . .

. . . and they both wear glasses.

After a good night's rest, Granny
was up early on Saturday morning.

'Morning all!

After breakfast, she went with
Simon, Josie and Monty
to the park.

In the afternoon she took them to the boating lake.

And in the evening she taught them a new card game.

This one's called 'Three Card Brag.'

So everyone was quite tired by the end of the day.

Granny Sprod was glad to get to bed, and soon fell asleep.

But at half past three in the
morning Granny Sprod woke up.
And feeling rather hungry . . .
she crept
downstairs
to get
a snack.

Granny Sprod had forgotten that
Monty slept in the kitchen.
She almost tripped over him as
she fumbled for the light switch.

Granny Sprod looked round, and
found the biscuit jar.

She helped herself to a biscuit.
Then she had another.
And then another.
Soon they were
all gone.

Munch
Munch

Then Granny Sprod turned out the
light, and went back to bed.
The house was quiet again.

In the morning, Mr Sprod noticed
lots of crumbs near Monty's basket.

Crumbs

Then he noticed
that the lid of
the biscuit jar
hadn't been
replaced . . .

Not
replaced

BISCUITS

Empty

. . . and then
he noticed
the jar was
empty!

'Monty!' he shouted angrily.
'It's very naughty of you to have
scoffed all the biscuits.'

Mr Sprod decided to teach Monty
a lesson. He told Monty that today
he'd have no breakfast.

Mr Sprod started cooking breakfast for Granny – sausages, bacon and scrambled eggs.

Monty's nose was twitching at the delicious aroma.

When Mr Sprod had finished
cooking breakfast, he took it up to
Granny.

Monty couldn't help following the
nice smell upstairs.

Granny Sprod had just woken up.
'Good morning, Mother!' said
Mr Sprod.

Mr Sprod gave Granny her
breakfast.
He didn't notice that Monty had
followed him into the room.

After Mr Sprod had left, Granny
looked at all the food.

Oh dear, I don't fancy this food after all those biscuits.

She put the tray on the floor.
'Hey, Monty, can you manage this?'
she asked.
Monty was happy to help out.

Mmm, Granny, you should come to stay more often!

Monty meets Bruiser

It was summer, and the Sprods
were off on holiday.
This year they were staying at:

BRIGHTSEA CAMPSITE

WAY IN

SHOP

WELCOME!
PLEASE
CHECK IN
ON ARRIVAL

XJ 121

After they'd checked in, Mrs Sprod
parked the car.
Mr Sprod helped her put up the
tent, while Simon and Josie
unloaded things from the car.

They noticed two children standing
by a nearby tent.
Monty noticed their ugly dog.

When the Sprods' tent was up and everything unpacked, Simon and Josie thought about what to do before tea.

'I think your father and I could do with a rest,' said Mrs Sprod.

So Simon and Josie went over and said hello.

Then they introduced Monty.

Amy and Alan introduced *their* dog.

Amy and Alan agreed on a game,
so they all went to the play area.

Bruiser was very clever at catching the Frisbee in his teeth.

Monty wasn't so good.

Bruiser could throw the Frisbee too.
He twirled his head round,
opened his jaws, and sent it flying.

'Bruiser must be the cleverest dog
around!' shouted Amy.

After the game, they all headed back to the campsite. Bruiser was feeling very proud.

Everyone on the campsite knows Bruiser!

Monty wished he was as good with a Frisbee as Bruiser.

Back at the tent, Mr Sprod was
cooking some sausages and beans.
He invited Amy and Alan for supper.

Mrs Sprod handed out some
paper plates.

Monty decided to show Bruiser
a thing or two.

He snatched a plate between his jaws and twirled his head round.

Monty's idea was to release the plate, and then chase after it and catch it before it landed.
Even Bruiser hadn't tried that!

So Monty let go of the plate.
But it didn't go in the direction
which he had planned.

Monty tried another plate.
He twirled his head extra fast.

But things went wrong again.
This time the plate landed on a fat
man's tummy.

THWACK!

Simon and Josie tried to stop Monty, but he was determined to have one last try. Monty twirled his head round and sent another plate flying.

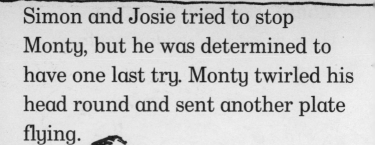

It went up and up . . .

and up . . . and up . . . and up . . .

A lot of people were wondering
where Monty's plate would land
this time.

The plate hovered on high . . .

. . . then amazingly . . .

. . . it headed back . . .

. . . like a boomerang!

Monty barked in excitement.

SMACK!

The plate landed right in Monty's jaws.

All the onlookers cheered.

Even Amy and Alan had to admit
that Monty was pretty unusual.

Only Bruiser looked unimpressed!

Monty's Big Surprise

One morning Monty was dozing when he heard Simon saying something about it being Monty's birthday.

Josie came over with a smile.

Monty was even more confused.

Monty wondered what the big
surprise could be.

A new basket?

A rubbber toy
to chew?

Or a plateful
of sausages?

Monty excitedly followed Josie outside. He could see Simon already waiting on the lawn. Monty was thrilled at the thought of a nice present.

But suddenly Monty's face dropped.
He spotted the soap, the scrubbing
brush and the bathtub full of water.

Oh no! Simon had been talking
about Monty's BATHday, not his
BIRTHday!

I think I'll get out of here!

Simon quickly grabbed Monty.

He popped Monty into the tub.

Brrrr! The water was freezing.

Monty didn't like being soaped all over by Josie.

And he *hated* the scrubbing brush.

Next came the rinsing down.

At last the ordeal was over, and
Josie hauled Monty out of the tub.

Now you're
spick and span,
Monty.

Monty stood near Simon and Josie
as they reached for a towel to dry
him with.
'I'll save them the trouble!' thought
Monty with a grin.
Suddenly Monty shook himself hard.
Water went everywhere!

Monty's Magic Trick

It was Christmas time and the Sprods were holding a party for Simon and Josie's friends. Mrs Sprod had made plenty of snacks – especially lots of tasty sausage rolls.

Everyone was enjoying the party.
Mr Sprod was doing a magic act
which all the children were
enjoying.

But Monty was getting impatient.
He couldn't stop thinking about the
sausage rolls in the kitchen.

During a rather long trick with a
disappearing egg, Monty thought
he could make some sausage rolls
disappear . . .

He got up and tiptoed towards
the kitchen.

But how could he get past Mr Sprod
without anyone noticing?

As Monty stood behind the table,
he spotted a big box on the floor.

It was halfway to the kitchen door.

Monty had an idea.

If I can reach that box, I can hide in there for a moment...

... and then when no one's looking...

...I can make a dash for the sausage rolls!

It seemed an easy enough plan.

Monty sneaked up to the box.

But as soon as he crept inside,
a secret flap went down and
everything went dark.

Monty was trapped in a secret
compartment.

Before Monty had time to escape,
he felt the box being
picked up.

Mr Sprod showed the box to the children. The inside was painted black, so it *looked* completely empty.

Mr Sprod put the box on the table, and tapped it three times with his magic wand.

Suddenly the secret flap moved.

Monty could see daylight again.

Without even looking in the box,
Mr Sprod pulled out . . .

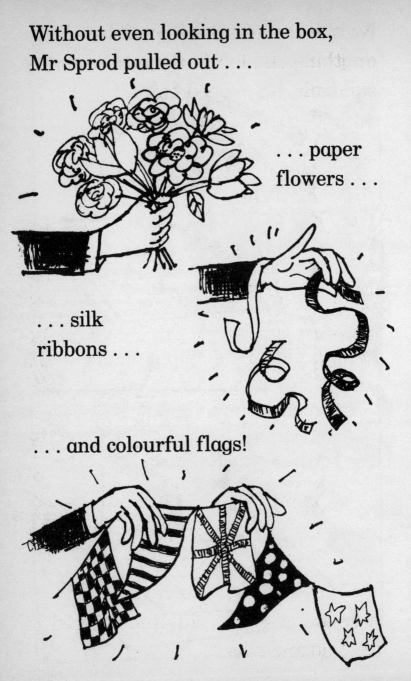

. . . paper
flowers . . .

. . . silk
ribbons . . .

. . . and colourful flags!

No one thought there could be
anything else left in the box, when
suddenly, up popped Monty!

Mr Sprod was as surprised as
everyone else. The children cheered
his amazing trick.

Just then, Mrs Sprod came in with
the sausage rolls.
Everyone tucked in.

That afternoon, Monty had more
sausage rolls than he'd ever eaten
before.
It was magic!